LITTLE BEAUTY

First U.S. edition 2008

Library of Congress Cataloging-in-Publication Data

Browne, Anthony, date.
Little Beauty / Anthony Browne. — 1st U.S. ed.
p. cm.
Summary: When a gorilla who knows sign language tells his keepers that he is lonely, they bring him a very special friend.
ISBN 978-0-7636-3959-4
[1. Gorilla—Fiction. 2. Cats—Fiction. 3. Animals—Infancy—Fiction. 4. Sign language—Fiction. 5. Human-animal communication—Fiction. 6. Zoos—Fiction.]
I. Title.
PZ7.B81984Lit 2008
[E]—dc22 2007051887

6 8 10 9 7 5

Printed in China

This book was typeset in Bookman.
The illustrations were done in pencil and watercolor.

Candlewick Press
99 Dover Street
Somerville, Massachusetts 02144

visit us at www.candlewick.com

LITTLE BEAUTY

Anthony Browne

CANDLEWICK PRESS

Once upon a time there was a very special gorilla who had been taught to use a sign language. If there was anything he wanted, he could ask his keepers for it using his hands. It seemed that he had everything he needed.

But the gorilla was **sad**.

One day he signed to his keepers,

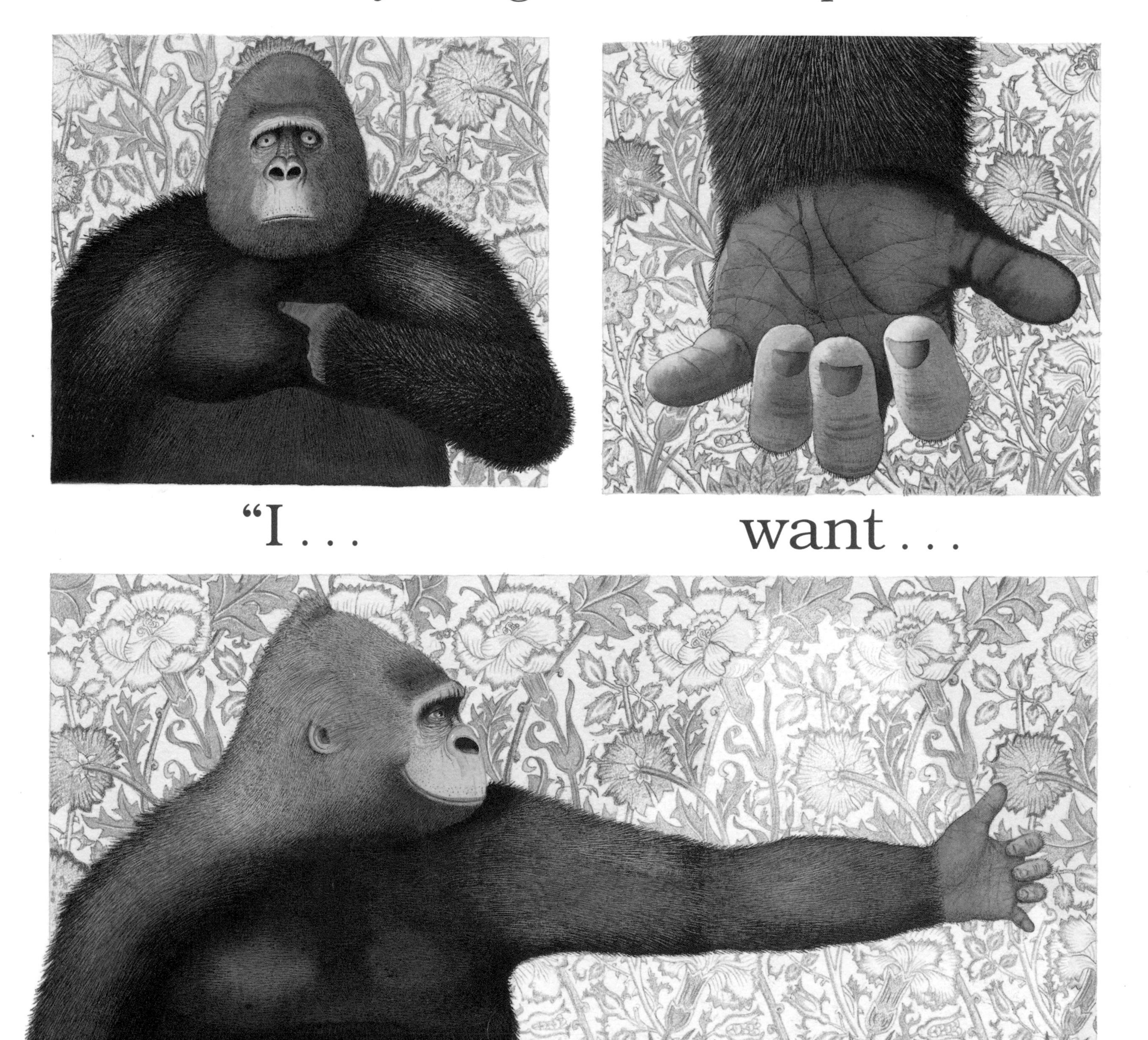

“I . . .

want . . .

a friend.”

There were no
other gorillas at
the zoo, and at first the
keepers didn't know what to do.
Then one of them had an idea.

They gave him a little friend

named Beauty.

“Don’t eat her,”

said one of the keepers.

The

gorilla

loved

Beauty.

He gave her milk

and honey.

They were happy.

They did **everything** together.

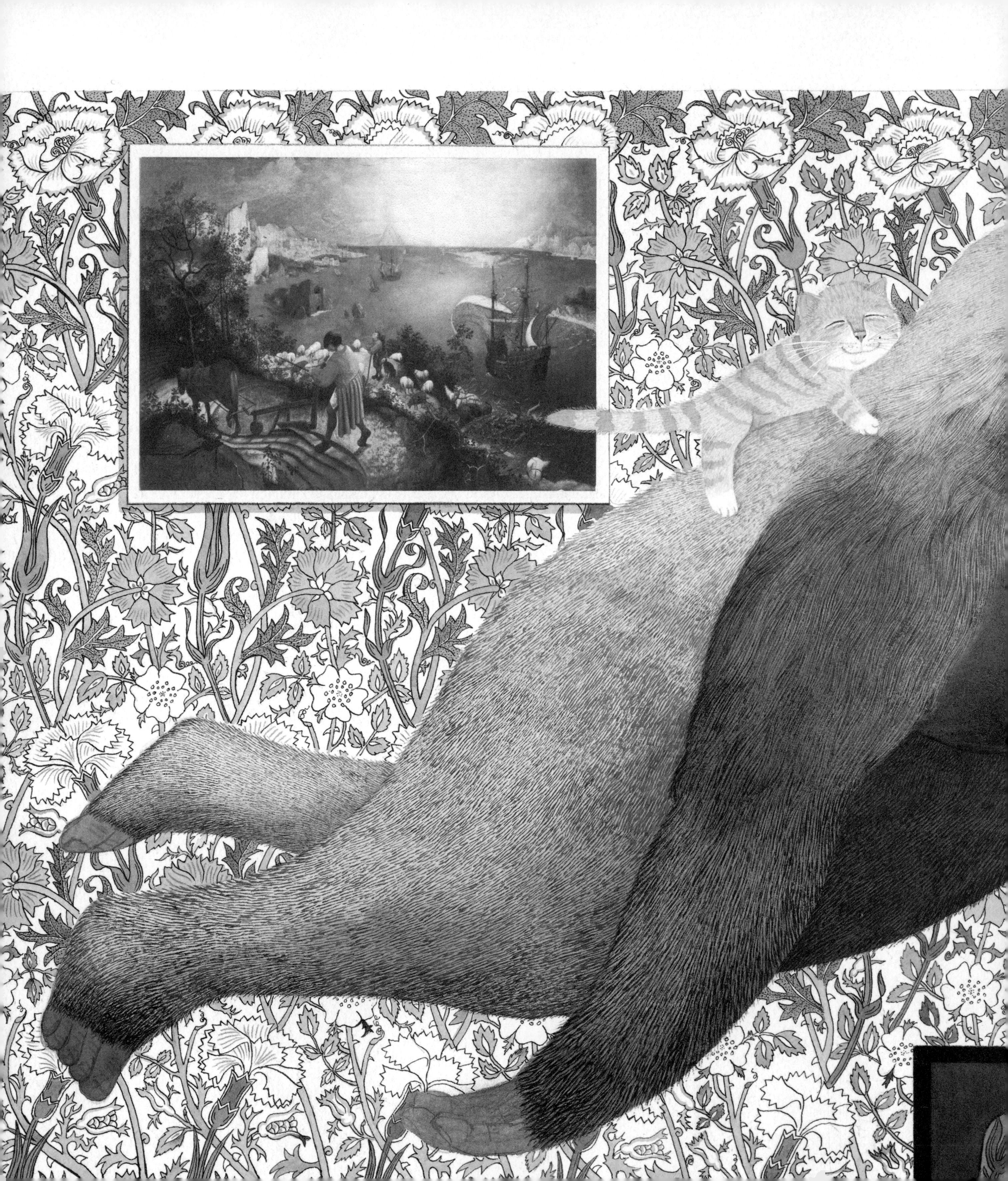

They were happy

for a long time . . .

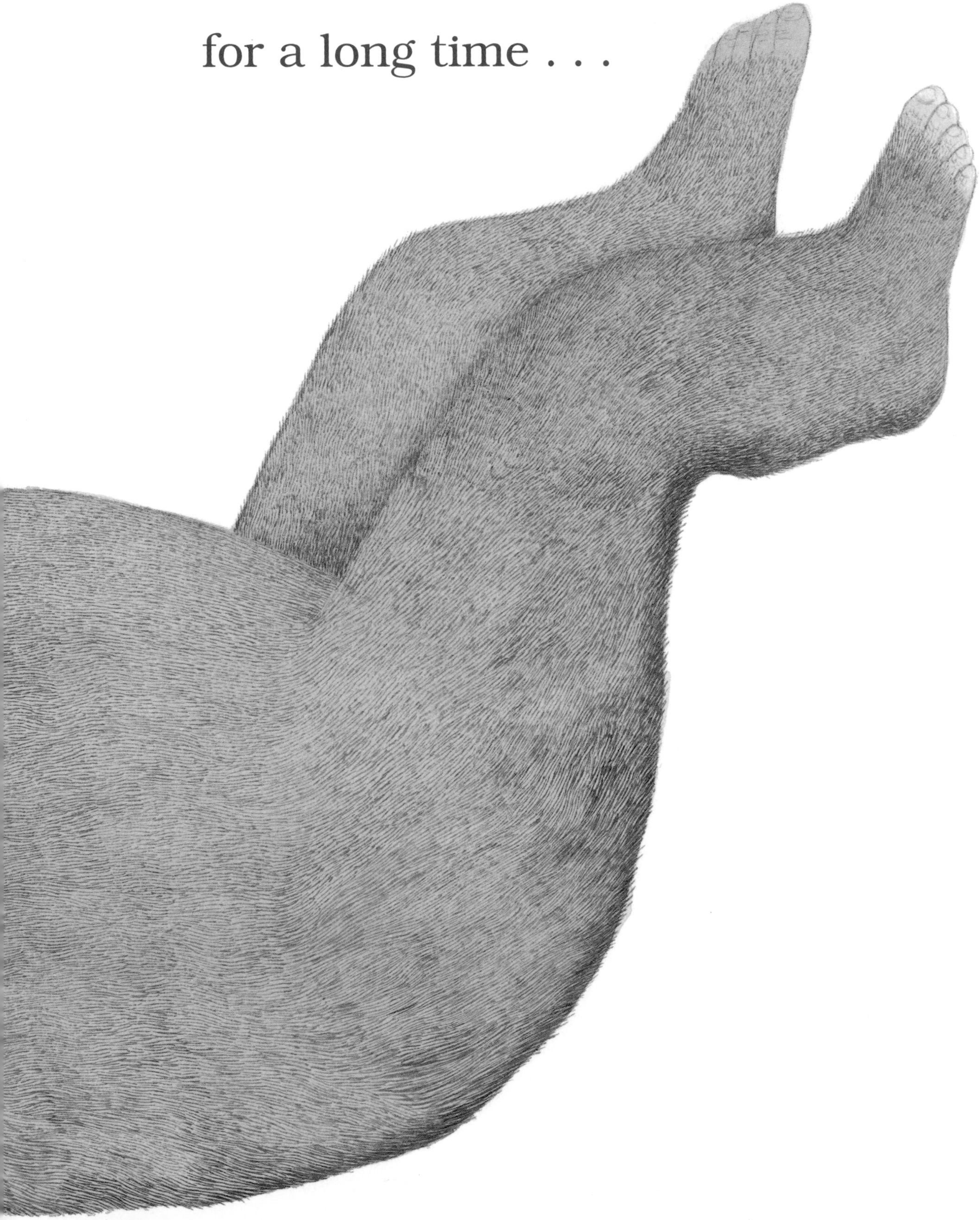

until one night when they watched a
movie together. The movie made
the gorilla very upset,

and

then

very

ANGRY!

The keepers rushed in.

“Who broke the television?” asked one.

“We have to take Beauty

away now,” said another.

The gorilla looked at Beauty.

Beauty looked at the gorilla.

Then Beauty started to sign . . .

"It . . .

was . . .

ME!

I broke

the television!"

Everyone laughed.

And do you know what happened?

Beauty and the gorilla lived

happily ever after.